PROPERTY of the NORTH POLE

Written by
WALLACE DIETZ

Illustrated by
CHRISTY MULLEN POPE

WALRUS BOOKS

Second Printing, 1998

ISBN 0-87517-095-1

WALRUS BOOKS

c/o Wallace Dietz
10717 Warren Rd.
Glen Allen, VA 23060

This book is dedicated to all the children and grown-ups who believe in the magic of Christmas and to Santa makers everywhere who use their hands to spread so much joy to others. Special thanks to Robert for all his technical help, Carlie for her editing, ideas, and encouragement, and everyone else who read this story and offered suggestions.

Lewis Brown of South Carolina carved the real Mustard Santa and Sande Elkins of Tennessee carved the real Santa with Stars. Many thanks to them for giving me permission to use their wooden figures as models for the Santa helpers.

CHAPTER I

"Ah-ooooga!" Michael had to bite his tongue to keep from hollering out loud. Christmas would soon be here. The clues were everywhere. Michael slid under his bed into his fort made of pillows, a blanket, and carefully stacked stuffed animals. Secretly, he took spy notes...

Just as Michael's parents came down the attic steps for a third time, his little sister shrieked with delight as she discovered him tucked away in his hiding place. "Billye!" shouted Michael. "Get out of my room!"

His cover blown, Michael silently slunk downstairs.

His parents passed going in the opposite direction without so much as uttering a word or glancing his way. This made perfect sense to Michael. After all, he had read enough about chameleons in his nature books to figure out some of their camouflage tricks.

A sly grin slowly made its way across his face as he crept closer and closer to his objective. With only minutes to spare before the treacherous villains would return, Michael, clutching his trusty ion space blaster, crawled on his belly across the living room rug right up to the piles of treasure. He hurriedly opened one of the dust-covered boxes, pulled away the tissue paper, and held up an old Santa Claus doll.

He was right! His head filled with visions of candy canes, houses and trees draped in cascades of colored twinkling lights, cookies shaped like Christmas trees decorated with icing and red and green sprinkles, stockings hung over the fireplace, overflowing with multi-colored balls of Ooey-Gooey-Kablooie bubble gum, popguns, wind-up robots, and.... Flooded with so much excitement, unable to contain himself, Michael burst into his Christmas dance (which looked a lot like his candy dance).

"Michael." His dad's voice popped his daydreams. "You can open up the boxes just as soon as we get the rest downstairs. Thanks for waiting."

Bamboozled! With all enemy weapons trained upon

his every movement, he knew the moment had passed to duck, roll, and find cover. The daring and cunning secret agent sensed his impending doom. With his head hanging down so low that his chin touched his chest, he grudgingly agreed to the terms of his shameful surrender.

As soon as Michael gently placed the last package on the floor, he flipped open one of the boxes labeled SANTAS. He eagerly searched for his favorite Santa figures from Christmases past: the Howling Santa, the Spinning Top Santa, the Sparkly Santa, the one that shook a bell, the Noah's Ark Santa, the Wind-up Santa, the Candy Container Santa, and the Santa Sitting on a Snowball. Michael and his dad would place these and other Santas haphazardly around the house, but it did not matter whether they put them here or there; Michael's mother would come behind them later to find just the right spot for each Santa.

Michael's parents announced that this was the day he could officially start his Christmas list. "Ah-ooooga!" hooted Michael. He no longer had to make his plans under his bed covers by flashlight. So after a vigorous and soap-bubbly scrub in the bathtub, Michael slipped into one of his dad's T-shirts and settled in by the snap-crackling fire. His mind was already on his next daunting task. With scissors, toy catalogs, and paste, he began working with a steely sense of purpose. There was no way Santa Claus would mess up his order this year, he thought to himself. He would make sure of this by attaching the pictures of what he wanted onto his Christmas list. He also decided to make a separate list for his grandparents, since he knew they would get him whatever he wanted. He even clipped out a coupon to make their shopping easier.

Choosing from the gadzillions of toys that he saw on TV, in department stores, and in catalogs that came by mail was proving to be a difficult job. Toys were bombarding him from everywhere! Did he want the Super Blooper Burp Gun with real live action fire that came complete with a commando belt that held 10 burp balls and had a built-in radio and secret compartment, or should he ask for the Rapid-fire Triple Barrel Assault Weapon that included an infrared scope and color-changing foam darts? He added both to Santa's list, since his mom would never consider these toys.

CHAPTER 2

At the gift shop the next day, Michael joined his family in the hunt for more Santas to add to their ever-growing collection. Michael spotted them first. He stared in awe at the three most unusual Santas he had ever seen. One had a snow globe where his stomach should have been, and inside the glass ball were cookies and several containers of milk. Another Santa, in a flying position, juggled three stars. Michael thought his red and green striped socks and polka-dotted mittens looked silly. The third one wore a mustard-colored coat and a grin from ear to ear. Could this be because the pack on his back was full of switches?

"Mom! Dad! Over here!" exclaimed Michael, never taking his eyes off his discovery.

His parents were speechless. His dad turned to his mom and said, "Honey, I think these three jolly guys have just found a new home."

Michael and his family whisked the carved wooden Santas away to the checkout counter where the cashier, who also happened to be the owner of the shop, remarked, "Oh. These are very special Santas."

"We've never seen any quite like these," chimed in Michael's mom.

"Well," continued the shop owner, "I think they are all

TREES
½ OFF

SPECIAL
PRICE
ON
SANTAS

one-of-a-kind. I found them the day after last Christmas buried beneath the snow behind my store. You can carry them home in the crate that I found them in if you would like."

"That's weird!" said Michael as he strained to read some words printed on one of the wooden slats of the crate. "It looks like this says PROPERTY OF THE NORTH POLE!"

Everyone laughed.

There was more, however, to these whimsical Santa figures than anyone could ever imagine.

CHAPTER 3

The next morning on the bus ride to school, Michael wrestled with so many burning questions that he felt like his head was on fire. Was there really a bearded, old, fat guy with a heart and chuckle as big as his waistline who traveled around the world spreading goodwill? Maybe the older boys at his school were right about Santa. The idea of an old man prancing around out in the cold, late at night, in his bright red pajamas sounded sillier and sillier the more he thought on it. There were other equally important questions as well. Just when did those TV cartoon characters go to the bathroom? And why did his mother insist that he clean his room when they both knew that he would just have to mess it up all over again?

All these questions and more evaporated as he neared the inviting entrance to Mrs. Waddill's classroom. He started to think how lucky he was to have a teacher who liked to do all the same things that he enjoyed doing such as identifying bones found in owl pellets and studying Venus, a planet hidden by a shroud of poisonous dust clouds.

Michael felt even luckier this morning because Mrs. Waddill had brought all the goodies needed to make gingerbread houses. Between gobbles, chomps, and chews, Michael used vanilla icing to attach graham crackers to a small milk carton. He spread more icing all over the outside of the crackers and stuck on so many candy canes, jawbreakers, gumballs, candy orange slices, gumdrops, and tiny sour tarts that one could barely see icing or crackers. For Michael, the best part of any construction project was usually devising the proper method of obliteration. He fought off his destructive urges and decided that his scrumptious candy-coated house would be better suited, at least for now, as scenery for the Santas at home.

Busy building and admiring his architectural masterpiece, Michael had paid little attention to the new boy in class, Jonathan, who sat directly across from him. As soon as Michael noticed that Jonathan had not yet begun building, Michael flicked a gumball across the table, hoping to catch his attention. Jonathan kept staring blankly at his pile of candy and crackers.

"Aren't you going to put together a gingerbread house?" asked an astonished Michael.

"I don't know," replied Jonathan glumly.

It was as if a dark nimbus cloud were hanging over Jonathan's head. For a brief second, Michael saw an opportunity to add to his stash of candy loot, but Jonathan appeared so sad that Michael became curious. He said to himself, "Doesn't he know that this is the season to be jolly? Fa-la-la-la-la la-la-la-la." The tune even rang in his head.

"Why are you so sad?" inquired Michael, not knowing what to expect for the answer.

After a heavy sigh, Jonathan spoke: "My parents told me that Christmas wouldn't be coming this year. My dad lost his job- we don't have any money for Christmas."

Michael didn't know what to say. He stayed quiet for the rest of the school day.

On his return home from school, he plopped down by the sparkling Christmas tree to put the finishing touches on his Christmas list, but something just wasn't right. He couldn't put his finger on what was bothering him, but he just didn't feel like working on his list anymore.

CHAPTER 4

Christmas Eve finally came. Michael was so excited that his fingertips and feet tingled. With rabbit-like twitches of his nose, Michael stood near the Christmas tree and sniffed and whiffed, savoring every molecule of the sweet pine aroma. Every now and then his Christmas bliss was interrupted by some nagging doubts. He had heard all the rumors and rumblings, so he was determined to prove once and for all, beyond a shadow of a doubt, that there really was a Santa Claus. The wheels and gears turned so rapidly and steadily in his brain that, if one listened closely, he could clearly hear the whirring and clicking noises.

Minutes later, a smile overtook Michael's face - the kind of smile that meant he had an idea - a big one. He waited for his parents to turn their lights off and settle into bed. When all was quiet, he crept downstairs to accomplish his secret mission. Under the watchful eyes of the dozens of Santa figures scattered about the living room, Michael set up an elaborate web of strings tied ankle-high from chair to table to chair to sofa to chair. The plan was foolproof. He knew a good trap when he saw one because he'd had lots of practice over the years using his sister's favorite toys to lure her into one devious trap after another. So when an unsuspecting Santa Claus innocently walked across the room to place Michael's presents under the tree, there would be no way he could avoid running into one of the strings. And since each string that connected the furniture was tied to other strings that were all attached to the Christmas tree, the tree would come crashing down, sounding the alarm that Santa Claus had arrived.

His task completed, Michael stepped back, looked approvingly at his handiwork, and scurried up the steps to his bedroom. He loaded and placed his favorite and most fearful weapon, a Rebel Series Gunk Catapult Launcher, on the floor beside his bed. He affectionately referred to this gun as his "oozie" because gunk was an oozing, slimy, sticky, jellyfish-like substance. Michael had even modified his catapult launcher by replacing the original Ping-Pong sized firing dish with one large enough to fire a plastic-coated glob of gunk the size of a softball.

Since Santa Claus was supposed to be quick for his size, Michael slept fully clothed so there would be no delays when the trap was sprung. As he lay on his bed wrapped up like an egg roll in his sleeping bag, he wondered if Santa Claus really looked like the pictures he'd seen in the books that he'd read. Being extra tired from the night's covert activities, Michael quickly drifted off to sleep.

CHAPTER 5

Each tick of the clock brought midnight and Christmas closer and closer. The Christmas spirit, already hanging rich and heavy in the chilly night air, swelled as more people showered their fellow man with gifts of love and kindness. As the magic increased, it started to course through the veins of the three Santa figures recently purchased from the gift store. The wooden carvings, brimming with enchantment, sprang to life, awaking from a yearlong snooze.

The Santa juggling the stars was the first to stir. "Where are we?" he wondered aloud as he removed himself from his stand. He pulled his three stars off the wire skewer and placed them in his coat pocket.

"I'm not sure where we are," answered the still groggy Santa Snow Globe, rubbing his eyes.

"Is Santa Claus waiting on the rooftops for us?" asked the Mustard Santa, adjusting his backpack full of sticks.

The Santas stood in place and scanned the room. They became even more confused when they noticed the dozens of other Santas scattered about, covering the fireplace mantle, the cupboard shelves, and the tabletops. They all had the same thought: "Who are these guys?"

"Hey you!" said the Santa with Stars, poking his finger

into the oversized tummy of the Santa doll standing behind him. "Look lively! Santa Claus could be back any moment. On your toes!" he commanded.

The Santa doll didn't even move or change his expression.

"I don't think these Santas are real," spoke the Mustard Santa as he tugged gently on the rabbit fur beard of a Santa sitting on a snowball.

"Well, let's be sure," said the Santa Snow Globe who proceeded to stomp with all his might on another Santa's big black boots.

All the Santa figures that surrounded them remained motionless.

The three puzzled Santas looked at each other and shrugged their shoulders. They glanced to the right, then to the left. Convinced that it was safe, they hopped off the top of the cupboard, landing knees bent on the rug below. At that time, the Santas noticed the stacks and stacks of presents around the Christmas tree. They had never seen so many presents left behind for children.

"This has to be a mistake," whispered the Santa Snow Globe, knowing that if someone or something heard them that they would be easy targets.

"I bet I know why Santa Claus has left us here," interrupted the Santa with Stars. "He's made a mess of things, leaving too many packages for one family, and he wants us to fix it for him. I bet he's waiting on the rooftop right now, wondering why we're taking so long retrieving these extra presents."

"Let's get them and cram as many as we can up the chimney!" shouted the Santa Snow Globe, readying himself to lead the charge and forgetting how vulnerable they were on the open floor.

All three Santas sprang into action, racing toward the tree. Suddenly, to their great surprise, the tree tilted in their direction. The unwitting Santas had sprung Michael's booby trap! They had to dive out of the way to avoid being crushed by the....CRASH!!!!

tinkle....

tinkle....

tinkle....

The sound of glass ornaments shattering vibrated through the house long after the tree had fallen. The tree quivered as it rested on the floor.

CHAPTER 6

Michael shot up from his cozy sleep, grabbed his Gunk Catapult Launcher, and dashed down the stairs. He stopped abruptly before reaching the entrance to the living room. This was the ultimate moment of truth. His stomach turned somersaults… he gasped for a big breath of air. Cautiously, he peered into the room. He did not see a thing, yet he heard the faint pitter-patter of footsteps. With a trembling voice, he half-heartedly ordered, "S-s-stop or I'll sh-shoot!"

He heard more steps and saw several packages scooting across the room, seemingly under their own power, toward the fireplace. Fear ran through every nerve in his body as he imagined that Santa Claus must be a ghost! He pulled the trigger and lobbed a gelatinous glob of gunk. SPLATTTT! His first shot, sailing high above its intended target, splattered against the white wall.

The packages stopped moving. With trembling hands, Michael turned the knob on the side of his gun. By adjusting the setting from 'stun' to 'vaporize,' he increased the tension on the spring that powered the launcher. He pulled the firing dish back until it locked in place with a click, grabbed another gunk ball from his pocket, and plopped it into the firing dish. With newfound confidence, he spoke up: "OK. No more funny stuff!"

His brain raced, searching desperately for something to say that would strike fear into the heart of his invisible enemy. He wished that he could remember the type of things that his favorite superheroes said in similar situations. "Get your hands off my presents!" was the best he could muster.

The stunned Santas, sensing that the game was over, stepped away from the gift-wrapped packages behind which they were cowering. Michael strained his eyes, trying to make out the details of three small, shadowy figures. It was then that he regretted leaving his infrared night vision goggles up in his room. Michael took three steps closer to the tiny figures. He shook his head in disbelief. In his wildest dreams, he had never imagined that Santa Claus would be such a shrimp, much less three shrimps!

"Where are you going with my presents? You're supposed to be delivering, not stealing!" blurted Michael, protective of his Christmas loot.

Still jittery, the Santas were at a loss for words.

"Who are you?" demanded Michael, getting angrier by the moment.

Regaining his senses first, the Mustard Santa spoke up nervously: "W-we are S-santa Claus' helpers. W-we're here to help S-santa Claus make his t-toy deliveries."

Still suspicious, Michael moved in another step. "Then why were you trying to shove my presents back up the chimney?" The finger on the trigger of his catapult launcher tightened slightly.

The Santa with Stars, whose nerves still jangled, spoke bluntly: "Santa Claus is on the roof waiting for us. He left too many presents here, and he wants us to bring some back to his sleigh to share with other children. No kid should get this many presents!"

Michael took another impatient step forward. By the light of the still blinking Christmas tree, he could now see that these were the Santa figures that his parents had purchased from the gift store a few weeks ago. Michael released his trigger finger and let out a slightly nervous chuckle.

"Santa Claus is not on this rooftop, and he did not send you to take my toys. I know because I was there when my parents bought you in a store. The lady who owns the store said she found you in the alley way under a pile of trash!" When he wanted to, Michael could be downright smart-alecky.

The Santas were shocked. Abandoned by Santa Claus? What had they done to deserve such a cruel fate? The Santa Snow Globe, already woozy from dodging a prickly tree and a glob of gunk, felt so weak from hearing the bad news that he collapsed.

"Does this one talk too?" asked Michael, picking up the Santa Snow Globe and shaking him the same way he always shook his double-thick-frosted chocolate malt drink. Michael wanted to see the snow swirling around the milk and cookies encased in the glass globe.

"Stop! Put me down!" screamed the Santa Snow Globe, who felt even queasier from the water tossing and swirling in his stomach.

"First tell me how you can walk and talk!" demanded Michael.

The dizzy Santa Snow Globe stumblingly replied: "We were…well…uh…we were whittled from…um…one of Santa Claus'…uh…Christmas trees, and…um…we come to life whenever…well… whenever there's enough magic in the air."

With his hands still clamped around the seasick Santa's sloshing mid-section, Michael lifted him up to eye-level for a closer look. Michael's eyes darted up and down and side to side, searching in vain for wires, a battery compartment, a wind-up key, or an on/off switch. Keeping his grip tight, Michael continued his investigation, flipping the Santa upside down.

"That's enough! Put him down! If Santa Claus finds out you've been roughing us up, you can kiss the rest of your Christmases goodbye!" warned the Santa with Stars, stomping in his stocking feet.

Michael set the Santa down. He had become so fascinated with these Santa figures that he was not angry with them any more for trying to scatter his presents around the globe to children who weren't getting as many. Maybe there were even some children not getting any presents this Christmas. That thought saddened him. Then it hit him like those yellow jackets did last summer when he covered up their hole in the ground with his foot. For the last couple of weeks, something was really disturbing him deep down inside, yet for some reason, he had not been able to fathom what it was. It had become harder for him this Christmas to fully enjoy all the things that he had enjoyed so much in the past. Making his list had lost its luster. The cookies weren't quite as flavorful. The Christmas music was not as spine tingling. Further proof that something was amiss came from the tears that unexpectedly trickled down his face when the other reindeer didn't allow Rudolph to join in their reindeer games. Hiding behind the sofa during the Abominable Snowman scenes was typical, but

crying was definitely new territory for Michael.

"I'm not gonna hurt you," assured Michael. He sat down so that he would be eye to eye with the three Santas. "If you really are Santa Claus' helpers," continued Michael, lowering his voice, "then maybe you all can help me with something." Each Santa leaned forward, ear first. "There's a boy at my school named Jonathan, and his mom and dad don't have the money to buy anything for Christmas. Do you want to go with me to take some of my presents to his house?"

Well, since the Santas had nowhere else to go, they agreed without hesitation. Once again, they began the task they had started earlier in the evening before being so rudely interrupted. The Santas immediately started cramming presents into the fireplace. The Santa with Stars placed his hands and feet against the inner walls of the chimney, positioning himself to shimmy upwards.

"Let's just use the front door," suggested Michael. With no argument, they all skittered out the doorway, loaded down with packages of all shapes and sizes.

CHAPTER 7

By porch light, Michael and the Santas piled the gifts for Jonathan in Michael's dependable wagon. Michael strapped his catapult launcher across his back and rolled the wagon away from his house. He now noticed how dreadfully cold and dark it was outside. Thick, billowy clouds so completely blanketed the night sky that no moon or stars could be seen.

"I can't see a thing," said Michael with a worried look on his face.

"No problem," assured the Santa with Stars. He reached in his coat pocket and pulled out a glowing star, which pulsated like the dying embers of a campfire. "Which way to Jonathan's house?" he asked with an air of confidence.

Michael was able to recall where Jonathan lived because Jonathan rode the same bus to and from school. When Michael pointed out the way to Jonathan's house, the Santa threw his star in that direction. The star swooshed through the air like a flare, spitting and hissing, leaving a trail of smoke, sparks, and flame. But unlike the fireworks that Michael had seen on the Fourth of July, this ball of flames stayed suspended in the air, lighting the way ahead of them.

Not accustomed to walks of any distance, the Santas

decided to ride in the wagon with the gifts. While they gingerly boarded, Michael, as if sipping thirstily from a straw, sucked in the cold night air. He imagined that there were a dozen tiny butterflies, fluttering about wildly in his tummy. With this tingling sensation sweeping throughout his body, he set out on his journey with his new companions, using the star to guide him.

Michael pulled the wagon across the front yard of his

next door neighbor's house. Immediately, the Santas began complaining loudly about the bumpy ride and begged him to take the roadway. He ignored their hullabaloo, however, because his parents didn't allow him to walk in the street. Slightly regretful of his decision to invite the babbling Santas, Michael continued to cross from one yard to another, passing lifeless gardens, bushes, and trees. The foursome trekked on for several blocks, careful to avoid

cars parked in asphalt and gravel driveways, footballs and basketballs left outside from the day's play, and the cats that came out to investigate all the commotion.

When they arrived at Jonathan's gray, stucco house, they faced another challenge. How were they going to get into the house to deliver the goods? Sadly, nobody left his doors and windows unlocked anymore. The Santas and Michael puzzled over what to do. Michael repeatedly flicked both of his ears with his index fingers. This is what he did sometimes to trigger a brainstorm. After minutes of ear-flicking, a mischievous grin stretched across Michael's face. Having never seen this expression before, the Santas waited eagerly to hear this little boy's plan.

Michael's plan was uncharacteristically simple. He proudly decreed that he would use his catapult launcher to fling each Santa up on the roof. Michael removed the unused gunk ball from the firing dish. Since he hated to see a perfectly good gunk ball go to waste, he forced it into his pocket.

After he rounded up the fleeing Santas, Michael stuffed one into the firing dish. One protesting Santa - zzzing! - after another - zzzing! - sailed through the air - zzzing! - and landed with a clutter-clatter on the rooftop. Michael watched as the Santas, muttering something about insurance policies, limped and hobbled to the house's chimney.

The Santas leaned over the rim of the smokestack,

peering down. Michael guessed that there must be yet another problem, because the Santas, after several minutes, still stood in their same spots. It looked like they were arguing. Michael shook his head in disgust and silently wondered how Santa Claus ever made all his deliveries with such bungling help.

"Maybe Santa Claus did leave them behind on purpose," he considered, knowing fully well that at the rate things were going tonight, he might have to do the same. (He thought about using his last gunk ball to blast them off the roof before they ruined his plan.)

The wisps of smoke coming from the chimney told the Santas that shimmying down would be dangerous. Santa Claus had always carried a container of water with him to douse out the remnants of any fires that might endanger him or his helpers.

"Oh this is great," said the Santa with Stars sarcastically. "I'm not burning my britches. Someone else go first!" he added, wondering which one he should push down the chute.

"I know," said the Santa Snow Globe. He turned to the Mustard Santa. "Take one of your sticks and use it to break open my glass globe. We can put this fire out with the water inside my stomach."

"But that might hurt," warned the Mustard Santa, not liking the idea of hitting anyone for any reason.

"I've been wanting to get at those cookies all night. I'm starved!" admitted the Santa with the Stars. Before anyone else could react, he snatched a sturdy stick from the Mustard Santa's backpack and took a mighty and forceful whack at the glass globe that beckoned him.

The glass shattered. Water streamed through the cracks in the sphere. They could hear the sizzling sounds below, and a big puff of smoke and ash signaled that it was safe to descend.

Seconds later, after high stepping over some still hot coals in the fireplace, they made their way down a dark and narrow hallway, bumping into and tripping over each other. At the end of the passage, they climbed up on each other's shoulders. The Mustard Santa, who stood on top of the stack, unlocked and opened the front door. When they appeared in the open doorway, the Santas were still chewing on their cookies.

CHAPTER 8

Since time was of the essence in this operation, everyone lined up quickly between the wagon and the front entrance to Jonathan's house. The Santas and Michael passed the gifts from one to another. After the last present was deposited just inside the doorway, Michael decided that he wanted to leave a Christmas message for Jonathan and his family. He dumped all thirty sticks out of the Mustard Santa's backpack, dropped to his knees, hunched over, and began spelling out his greeting with great concentration. The Mustard Santa knelt down beside Michael, watching him with curious admiration. The Santa Snow Globe cupped his hands over his ears to listen for any sounds coming from the bedrooms while the Santa with Stars, who stood by the front door, whistled an 'any time now' song. Michael's hands flitted like wild birds, moving the sticks to form letters.

was as far as Michael could get.

"Hmmmm," Michael was thinking out loud. After a short flurry of ear-flicks, the solution dawned on him.

Michael rearranged the sticks to complete his message…

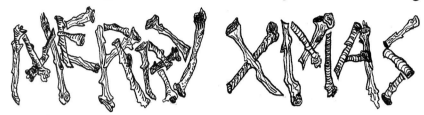

Their mission accomplished, they scrambled out the doorway. By the safety of the wagon, the Santas patted each other on the back, and Michael congratulated them for a job well done by showing them how to 'slap-five' high and low. Then something wonderful and rare happened. Michael's kind deed pushed the clouds, already waterlogged with the magic spirit of Christmas, past their saturation point. Snow began to fall. The four friends celebrated with somersaults and headstands until they fell to the ground in exhaustion. By the time they reached Michael's house, a soft fine powder covered everything.

Weary from all the excitement, everyone trudged into the living room to a spot in front of the fireplace. "I guess this is goodbye," Michael said, choking on his last word. The three Santas nodded. Michael's eyes swelled with tears. He hugged and said farewell to each of his new friends, who for the first time tonight were silent. In a gesture that Michael thought was strange, the Santa with Stars, the Mustard Santa, and the Santa Snow Globe knelt down in front of him. With several blinks of Michael's bleary eyes, they vanished. Michael giggled because he thought he could

hear the faint sounds of bickering and complaining as the jostling Santas shimmied up the chimney to await Santa Claus' arrival on the rooftop.

Michael slowly lumbered up the stairs and burrowed under the snug covers of his bed. He felt good knowing that Jonathan would find presents and a Christmas greeting when he woke up in the morning. What seemed to be a low voltage of electricity surged throughout his body, causing all the hair on his arms, legs, head, and back of the neck to rise on its end. He pictured himself as a giant moray eel, swimming through the sea grass, chasing squid. Something weird was happening. He'd given up some of his own toys, yet he was feeling ecstatic. His bed had never felt as warm and welcoming as it did this night.

CHAPTER 9

When the first gray light of Christmas day peeped into his bedroom window, Michael awoke and peeled away his covers. The movement he heard downstairs meant that his parents had seen the fallen tree, the crushed ornaments, the big empty spot on the rug where his presents should have been, and the gunk glob plastered on the wall. Ridden with guilt, Michael imagined that the force of gravity had tripled. He trudged in slow motion down the stairs, each step growing heavier and heavier until he stood in front of his father, mother, and sister in the living room.

The suspicious glares zeroed in on him. "What?" he uttered innocently, attempting to wiggle out of this tight spot. All ears waited for an explanation. "What!?!?" he spoke more forcefully, hoping that if he sounded a bit miffed, they would look elsewhere for a suspect. He reluctantly lifted his eyes from the floorboards to view a room full of incriminating evidence. Foreheads frowned at him, demanding an explanation. "What!!!!" he shouted, squirming in agony. He finally cracked, confessing fully - well, not quite because he doubted that his parents would believe that three Santa figures had come to life. Thus, he took the blame for everything - even knocking the tree over. He further explained that he'd felt so sad for a new student at his school named Jonathan that he'd taken some presents over to his house late last night so that Jonathan would have a Christmas, too. He finished and waited.

Dad looked serious. His face squinched up. His mother's jaw trembled. His sister bit her lower lip to keep from laughing.

"Uh, oh! Here it comes!" he worriedly thought to himself. He visibly cringed as he awaited the onslaught. "What method of torture would they concoct?" he wondered, shrinking some more. The last time he felt this way was when he sawed off the legs to his sister's bed.

Michael's dad placed a hand on Michael's shoulder. "Thanks, Michael," he said sincerely, "for reminding us what Christmas is truly all about."

His teary-eyed mom hugged him and kissed him on the cheek. He promptly wiped his face clean but told his mom he was rubbing the kiss in.

Michael watched in amazement as his parents gathered up their gifts and placed them by the front door. He still wasn't sure what was happening even as he was helping to cover the pots and pans of food intended for his family's big midday feast. He sealed a big disgusting bowl of green peas with plastic wrap and transported this and other containers of food to his dad's station wagon. Like most children, he thought his parents were a little weird, but having their special Christmas meal in the car was taking things too far.

Once the car was loaded, Michael's dad hollered, "All aboard!" Everyone scrambled to find a place to sit among all the presents and food. After a chorus of "Buckle up!" the station wagon lurched forward. Michael's ears filled with the thick crunching of fresh snow and the clitter-clattering of the pots and pans knocking about in the back compartment. The incessant chattering of pots and their lids reminded him of his noisy Santa friends.

He wondered if the rascally Santas were simply a part of some weird dream he had had last night. With his house still clearly in view, he looked up on the roof to see if the Mustard Santa, the Santa Snow Globe, and the Santa with Stars were still up there. There were no Santa figures in sight.

"Wait a minute!" His disappointment changed to joy when he saw the Christmas message scraped in the snow on top of the roof.... MERRY X-MAS spelled with an 'X'. Michael's face beamed with a knowing smile as last night's adventure started to replay in his head.

"Michael." The pictures flashing in his brain dissolved like a wad of cotton candy placed in a watery mouth.

"Michael," his dad repeated, "which way to Jonathan's house?"

Michael looked out his side window. Realizing that they were rapidly closing in on their destination, he shouted,

"Hold it!"

The station wagon came to a sliding halt in front of Jonathan's house. Michael and his sister hopped and skipped to the front door stoop with their parents trailing behind. When Jonathan and his family answered the door, the sight of Michael's family bearing gifts overwhelmed them. Not sure whether to laugh or cry, they did both. Michael and his family entered and the door shut behind them.

The house lit up like a Christmas tree, giving off a soft, warm, and welcoming glow.

THE END

EPILOGUE

Because of all the confusion in the morning, Michael had missed seeing the large box wrapped with shiny red paper and topped with a flowering, green bow. He found it tucked under the branches at the base of the Christmas tree, which he and his parents were just getting around to setting back up. He read the tag attached, which simply said "MICHAEL" written in the most elaborate script he'd ever seen.

In one crackling swoop, Michael ripped the paper off the mysterious package. He excitedly lifted and fumbled the lid. Inside were the Mustard Santa, the Santa with Stars, and the Santa Snow Globe in their stiff wooden forms. The snow globe had even been repaired. A note at the bottom of the box read:

Michael,

I thought I had lost my helpers forever! On returning to the North Pole last Christmas, a sharp blast of wind knocked the crate containing them off my sleigh. I didn't realize my magical carvings were missing until I was home and started to unpack.

Well, thanks so much for looking after them. You keep them for now, though. They're way too much trouble and I still have many more packages to deliver tonight. Your real present is under your bed. Merry Christmas and thanks for your help.

HO! HO! HO!

Love,
Santa Claus

"Ah-ooooga!" hooted Michael.